The
Bug Collector

Wrath James White

To Mom

TRIGGER WARNING!

This book is a work of Extreme Horror. It contains lewd, lascivious, and grotesque depictions of extreme violence, torture, dismemberment, disfigurement, murder, intercourse, premarital sex, fellatio, cunnilingus, analingus, anal intercourse, sexual abuse, child sexual abuse, sexually transmitted infections, disease, rape, cannibalism, prostitution, sexist language, homophobic language, racist language, foul language, threatening language, kidnapping, bondage, vomit, female ejaculation, golden showers, dysfunctional households, bad parenting, and the blatant misuse of kitchen utensils and chess pieces.

ACKNOWLEDGMENTS

Thanks to Shane Mosley, Lucas Mangum, and my son, Sultan Kai White, for their support and encouragement as I penned this nasty piece of work. To Monica J. O'Rourke for her mad editorial skills and for letting me borrow a scene from one of her stories. To Lisa Lee Tone for her invaluable assistance identifying all my usual mistakes. And to Todd Clark for beta reading and catching the little things.

"Bug Catching":

A fetish involving the act of collecting as many STDs/STIs as possible.

—Urban Dictionary

PROLOGUE
ULCERATIVE BUMPS AND BLOODY LESIONS

I was freezing. The chill wind raked across the ruin of my face with icy talons, like being slowly flayed by an invisible bird of prey. My fingers, toes, and ears were almost completely numb yet still throbbed with a penetrating bone-deep ache that promised an agonizing thaw once I got someplace warm. *If* I got someplace warm. It was nineteen degrees outside, which, for Las Vegas, was like twenty below. At gusts of thirty miles an hour, the windchill factor must have dropped the temperature at least another ten degrees.

The blustering gale pushed my emaciated form to and fro, threatening to toss me into the dense lackadaisical flow of traffic on the Las Vegas Strip. I imagined a twenty-mile-per-hour vehicular manslaughter, my fetid corpse slowly ground beneath the wheels of a rented sports car or limousine or perhaps a minivan driven by some happy suburban family enjoying their first vacation in years. I imagined gamblers and tourists gawking in slack-jawed horror. I could almost envision the neon lights reflecting off a slick red streak of my blood, my glistening viscera illuminated in the headlights of the surrounding traffic. Car horns blaring, imploring the emergency responders to quickly scrape my carcass off the asphalt so the tourists could resume their party. It wasn't an unpleasant thought at this point. I was tired. My body hurt. My fetish had destroyed my health and ruined my life. I was a victim of my own paraphilia.

A tattered wool blanket I'd acquired from a schizophrenic homeless woman I fucked behind a convenience store dumpster less than an hour ago was my only protection against the chill wind. I wrapped the stinking urine, semen, feces, and vomit-stained blanket tight around my shoulders and shuddered as another gust of wind knocked me back on my heels. I ducked my head into that arctic blast in an effort to make myself more aerodynamic.

The homeless woman I borrowed the blanket from had been a surprisingly good fuck and had no doubt provided a few more bugs for my collection, probably no more than chlamydia and crabs, but beggars can't be choosy. The best lays are always the crazy ones. Something about utter insanity makes sex wilder. Her maturity and experience was an added bonus.

The entire time we spent furiously copulating in the stench and filth leaking from the dumpster in front of us, she kept calling me Billy. I later learned "Billy" was her high school sweetheart who'd perished in a motorcycle accident thirty years ago, and seeing my face, she thought he'd returned from the grave to lick the custard-like discharge from her rancid geriatric vagina. I was more than happy to help her play out this fantasy.

The saggy pockmarked gooseflesh of her thighs, striped with varicose veins and wrinkled with age, parted like an old creaky barn door that might fall off its hinges at any moment. The old bag lady reached out for me, cupping my face in her filthy talons, and guided my head down to that frothing maw.

"Oh, Billy. Oh, you make me feel so wonderful. I missed you so much," she crooned as I went to work, lapping at the scabby folds of her labia. I sucked a bulbous growth that I hoped was her clitoris into my mouth and began flicking it with my tongue, then vigorously licking it like I was trying to remove a stain.

"Oh, Billy! I'm cumming!" she shouted again and again as one orgasm tumbled like an avalanche over the next. Her many orgasms were accompanied by an explosive emission of fluid I was pretty certain was urine. I didn't mind. I'd had my fair share of golden showers.

After providing the haggard vagrant with what I deemed to be a respectable number of orgasms, I decided to take my own pleasure between her flabby, wrinkled ass-cheeks. If there were any other infections to acquire, I was pretty confident the murky depths of her colon was where they would be mined from.

I stood up and peered into the dumpster, looking for something I could use as a lubricant. The crazy bag lady took the opportunity to free my cock from my sweatpants and take it between her lips, warts, sores, blisters, and all. The sheer vulgarity of the act, her obliviousness and disregard for the state of my diseased genitalia, made the act somehow sexier, dirtier. I found a wasted bucket of half-eaten fried chicken and used the congealed chicken grease, my saliva, and whatever rot leaked from her vagina to ease my intrusion into her gaping, well-traveled anus.

I had become quite adept at identifying sexually transmitted diseases and infections. Just as a bird watcher can identify different species of birds, I recognized the subtle differences in taste, smell, and appearance between symptoms of chlamydia and gonorrhea and your garden variety yeast infection. I could tell the difference between a particularly virulent case of genital warts and the donovanosis that festooned the old woman's anus with ulcerative bumps and bloody lesions. I had the same bleeding ulcers all along the shaft of my cock. It gave new meaning to the colorful colloquialism "bumping uglies." There were few things uglier than what was transpiring between my dick and her ass.

"Oh, Billy! Billy, your cock is so huge! You're filling me up. I feel like I'm going to burst!"

Having no reason to disrupt her illusion, I played along and became her Billy right up until I ejaculated. I eased my cock out of her ass moments before I climaxed, and the old woman eagerly welcomed my shit-slickened cock back between her lips to accept my load of corruption, licking my thick semen from her chapped lips and smiling like the happiest woman on earth.

I reached down and pulled up my pants.

"Stay with me, Billy. Billy, please don't leave me again! Don't go!" the old woman implored me as I turned to leave.

I picked up the tattered blanket we'd just fucked on and wrapped it around myself.

"Sorry. I have to go. Billy has to go," I said in the most soothing voice my blighted lips and throat could muster, trying my best to be gentle, sympathetic to her madness. I stroked the wild nest of oily split ends on her scalp and then lay a tender kiss on her soiled forehead. One of the many sores and blisters on my lips burst like a zit and dribbled pus down into her eyebrows.

"Billy has to go now," I repeated as I turned to leave.

The old bag lady grabbed hold of the blanket and held it in a death grip. I continued walking, dragging her along the concrete several feet before I gave the blanket a quick tug, wresting it from her grasp and simultaneously pulling her off balance.

The old woman toppled to the concrete face first. Her skull hit the ground with a hard, juicy wet crack that made me wince.

"I'm sorry. I'm so sorry. Are you okay?" She wasn't moving.

A crown of dark red had formed around her skull. The old woman twitched a few times before lying still. I was about to check her pulse when she let out a load moan. I took that as confirmation that she was okay, alive at least, so I hurried out from behind the dumpster and crossed the parking lot, letting out a sigh of relief when I was back on Las Vegas Boulevard, surrounded by drunks and unlucky gamblers. I had a new blanket and who knew how many new diseases. It wasn't a bad transaction as these things go.

CHAPTER ONE
PUNCHES, HAMMERFISTS, AND SLAPS

I wasn't homeless myself, but you wouldn't have known it by either my appearance or my recent activities. I owned a nice house in Seven Hills I hadn't seen in months. A Range Rover I'd purchased two years ago sat in the parking garage of one of the casinos, if it hadn't been stolen or towed yet. It had been weeks since I'd driven it. Until three years ago, I had a successful career writing computer code. That felt like a lifetime ago. My obsession had taken over every aspect of my existence and driven me to madness, though not yet poverty. Only of the spirit. I still had thousands of dollars in my bank account, and my mortgage and all my other bills were on auto draft. It would last at least another six or seven months. Eventually, everything would be foreclosed upon and repossessed. It didn't matter. That life was over. I now dwelled in the dark alleys, sewers, and gutters with the indigent and the insane, the prostitutes, castoffs, and lepers.

The sluggish drunken glut of slow-moving pedestrians wrapped in expensive coats and designer jackets carried me along on a lazy tide. Their proximity raised my anxiety. They were all so clean, healthy, and wholesome with their pink cheeks and fat bellies. I felt like a pariah among them, a grotesque wraith haunting their pleasant vacations.

Occasionally, one of the tourists would take notice of me and visibly recoil, sneering in revulsion. Others regarded me with confusion, trying to make sense of the corruption and deterioration of my flesh, wondering if I was wearing a costume of some sort. I saw the fear bloom in their eyes like autumn roses as the possibility dawned upon them that I could be carrying some horrendous communicable disease they could catch from merely standing within arm's reach of me and breathing the same air. They covered their faces with their shirts or jackets and quickly hurried past. Some turned and pointed. A few took out their phones and tried to record me. I pulled my hood down and my blanket up to hide my disease-ravaged visage and pushed my way past them.

My face was a horror. Exposure to humanity's rich bounty of venereal infections had overcome my once comely features and left a ghastly fright mask. Bleeding scabs and pus-filled blisters, bumps and lesions, and craters of rot and decay had completely overcome whatever attractiveness I'd once possessed. My nose had been lost to syphilis several years ago. Only an unctuous chasm moist with snot remained in the center of my face. Herpes sores and ulcers blossomed on my lips and eyelids like wild red berries. So much blood and pus seeped from my countenance it felt as if my face had liquefied and was oozing its way down my neck, which wasn't far from the truth.

"Dude, look! A fucking zombie!" a teenaged girl yelled, pointing at me while hurrying to retrieve her phone from her designer purse to capture my degradation. I turned away and quickened my stride, hurrying from her sight.

I left the strip, fleeing the bright neon lights, the loud voices, loud music, loud traffic. In long, determined strides, I made my way up Tropicana Boulevard and, finding a cozy spot beneath a freeway underpass, curled up in that filthy blanket and went to sleep like a troll under a bridge.

I hadn't slept for long when I felt a crushing pressure on my chest. My arms were pinned to my sides, and I was being smothered with a rough cloth that smelled of chemicals. My eyes flew open. A beautiful, dark-skinned Black woman dressed like a fashion model from the 1970s was straddling my chest, pressing a rag to my face. A feeling of vertigo overcame me, and I felt like I would soon lose consciousness. She was smothering me. I couldn't breathe. Instinctively, I began to fight.

I swung a wild punch that connected with the woman's jaw and snapped her head back. The rag fell away from my face, and I was able to gulp in a couple of quick lungsful of air. The woman was still on top of me. I thrust my hips skyward to buck her off and then gave her a shove.

She fell into the dirt and immediately scrambled back over to me, plucking the rag from the dirt and smashing it back into my face.

I felt dizzy again. I gave her another shove and scrambled to my feet. "What the fuck is going on? Who the fuck are you?"

"Oh, you don't remember me, motherfucker? You don't remember me?" She wore a long faux leather coat with a faux fur collar that hung open, revealing a tight-fitting tan sweater beneath it and a tan leather miniskirt. She still had the rag clutched in her hand and was baring her teeth like a mad dog, snarling and hissing. She wasn't just insane, she was furious, out of her mind with rage, and I had no idea who she was or what ill I had caused her.

"No. I don't know who the fuck you are!"

"You motherfucker!" she growled, and then swung a kick that whizzed past my knees and thighs, burying her toes in my scrotum.

My guts twisted with pain and nausea. I dropped to my

knees, clutching my sore balls, and rolled on to my side in the dirt. She dived on top of me and began raining down punches, hammerfists, and slaps while straddling my waist. I tried to hit back, but lying half on my side and half on my back only freed up one arm to fight with. The other was pinned beneath me. I didn't have the leverage to throw anything significant. I was practically helpless against this woman's fury.

My eyes were bruised and cut and beginning to swell shut, but I could still see the beautiful brown amazon who was assaulting me, and I struggled to place her face. Was she a past lover? Possibly. There had been so many. Well into the triple digits. Two hundred or more, if I had to guess. Perhaps even three or four hundred. I had always been more of a lover than a fighter. But the ability to inspire orgasms wasn't a useful skill at the moment. For every weak punch I threw from the bottom, she landed three or four hard strikes from above with her full body weight and the force of gravity behind them. I felt my face swelling from the bruising she was giving me. Her fists were caked with blood, pus, and mucus from the myriad sores and lesions ruptured by her punches.

When she finally grabbed the chemical-soaked rag and placed it over my mouth and nose, the slow, creeping blackness, slipping into the soothing arms of Morpheus, was a blessing.

CHAPTER TWO

BLOOD, SEMEN, AND SOME YELLOW AND GREEN LIQUID

"Why?" That was her biggest question.

Her name was Tina, and I was her prisoner, bound in duct tape, strapped to a cheap camping chair in an abandoned warehouse far from the bustle of the strip or the banal normality of the chain retail stores and cookie-cutter production homes that occupied the landscape throughout the rest of the city.

The answer to her question was long and, frankly, pretty weird, and I knew it wouldn't make sense to her. But they say confession is good for the soul, and I had never told anyone about my unique paraphilia before, except for a girlfriend I'd once had in college. I wasn't expecting her to be understanding. She was going to torture and kill me no matter what I said. Syphilis had rotted something in Tina's brain, leaving only this incoherent fury, and I was helpless before her, soon to die and probably horribly. So why not tell her the truth and unburden myself?

Tina was tall, lean, and muscular, with long, platinum-blonde dreadlocks, high cheekbones, and lips like pillows. Her brown skin was smooth and almost shiny. Just looking at her, you'd never know she was sick. She was rotting from the inside out.

"I'm a bug catcher. My goal was never to spread diseases but to acquire them. I didn't mean to hurt you. You must have had a disease or infection I wanted."

Her angry face contorted in confusion. That marriage of rage and incredulity created the most peculiar expression. It was almost comical. Were it not for the pain I was in, I would have probably laughed, or at least spared a chuckle. But I was still in quite a bit of danger, and even though I was already terminal, being burned, skinned, and dismembered wasn't how I wanted to die.

"That don't make no fuckin' sense! Why would anyone want to deliberately catch a disease?"

"You never heard of bug catching? I would think that, in your profession, you would have come across a few of us."

"Motherfuckers like you always talkin' 'bout my 'profession' like it's something disgustin' I should be ashamed of when it wouldn't even exist if it wasn't for dirty bastards like you who just want to get their dicks wet and would rather pay for it than get it from their wives or girlfriends."

Tina's anger won out over the confusion, and she slapped me across the face with the razor strop she'd been using to sharpen her straight razor. Blood and pus flew from the myriad wounds, cuts, and suppurating sores and pustules on my face. She slapped me again, splitting my lip and filling my mouth with more blood than the blisters on my tongue and the insides of my cheeks were already weeping down my throat.

"So what the fuck is a damn bug catcher? Like catchin' butterflies and shit? What the fuck that got to do wit' me?"

I risked a blood-caked smile this time, spitting strawberry-colored phlegm and saliva and coughing a few times to clear my throat.

"No, not that kind of bug catcher. A bug catcher, in the slang vernacular, is someone with a paraphilia, a fetish for sexually transmitted infections, deliberately allowing themselves to be infected. Contracting HIV is the ultimate goal of bug catching. It's the piece de resistance, the grand prize. The problem for most bug catchers is that the journey toward the grand prize is littered with many other STDs. But that wasn't a problem for me," I said, beaming proudly. "I wanted them too. I wanted every sexually transmitted infection known and unknown to humankind. See, I'm not merely a catcher. I'm a collector."

Tina scowled in disgust and hocked a wad of phlegm at my badly wounded face. "What the fuck kind of sick white boy shit is that? And why you talkin' all fancy and superior wit' all those big words and shit? Tryna act like you ain't just say some nasty-ass, perverted-ass, triflin' and disgustin' ass shit!"

"This is just how I talk. I can try to dumb it down, but I thought that might be insulting."

Tina's nostrils flared. Her mouth twisted into a snarl. She reminded me of a feral cat, a cougar or lioness, as she lunged at me, hissing mad with rage. "Motherfucker, you gave me crabs, hepatitis, syphilis, herpes, AIDS, and who the fuck knows what the hell else! And you're worried about offending me? Fuck you!"

She kicked me in my enlarged and enflamed scrotum with her open-toed, spiked, stiletto boot. The sharp heel pierced my left testicle, and it exploded like a lanced boil. Blood, semen, and some yellow and green liquid the consistency of phlegm splattered her toes, my inner thighs, and splashed down onto the concrete floor. A gangrenous stench like rotten eggs and putrefied flesh wafted up from my crotch. A wave of pain and nausea rolled through my stomach, raising the gorge in my throat until I vomited all over myself, adding the fetid aroma of a half-digested *carne asada* burrito to my own gangrenous stench.

I vomited twice more and then began to dry heave as stomach-churning agony twisted my guts into knots.

Tina stood above me, smiling contentedly as she watched me suffer. I was screaming even while choking on my own vomit and spitting out chunks on the floor.

"Okay, that's enough. Stop all that cryin' and hollerin'! I said cut that shit out unless you want me to stab you in your other nut."

It took several long minutes of screaming and weeping before I regained control of myself.

"I–I didn't mean for you to get infected. I swear. I didn't mean to hurt anyone. It wasn't anything personal. It was an unavoidable consequence."

Tina's scowl twisted into a snarl, and I braced for another attack, trying to turn my knees inward to protect my remaining testicle but unable to move more than a few inches due to the duct tape binding my ankles and calves to the chair legs.

"Oh, so I was just some kinda collateral damage?"

"Precisely. I wasn't targeting you. I was targeting the diseases you carried. Did you know there are over thirty different bacteria, viruses, and parasites known to be transmitted through sexual contact? I wanted to be the first to get them all!"

Tina's face relaxed a bit, curiosity winning out over fury momentarily. "How many you got?"

I shrugged. I had honestly lost count. "Like most bug catchers, I was after the HIV virus. I was a junior in high school when I first heard about AIDS, and the minute I heard about it, I knew I would catch it. I knew that's how I would die. Everyone was marching and raising money for a cure, trying to put pressure on the government to find a cure, but I knew they weren't going to cure it. A disease that kills junkies and gays must have sounded like a godsend to those religious wingnuts, elitists, and homophobes who run this country. And the pharmaceutical companies were probably licking their chops at all the money they would make just treating the disease without curing it.

"That's why we still don't have a real cure. They can reduce the virus to undetectable levels, but only if you take their expensive medications for the rest of your life. It's a pretty sweet scam. Anyone with half a brain knew that's how it would be, but I didn't care. There was actually a profound relief, a sense of peace, knowing the exact manner, if not the date of my death. It was almost comforting."

"That's fucking insane! Why would any motherfucker want to catch AIDS? What the fuck is wrong with you nasty bastards?"

I shrugged. "The same reason people race cars and jump out of airplanes, I'd suppose. There's something exhilarating about flirting with death. But, when you rawdog some bus station skank or low-rent rent-boy, you don't really get to choose what infection you're going to walk away with. Yes, you may get HIV, but you might also contract chlamydia, gonorrhea, syphilis, herpes, hepatitis, genital warts, and a host of other STIs far more virulent than the HIV virus. And with so many people on medications that suppress the virus to a level that makes it undetectable and therefore un-transmittable, it was less and less likely that bug catchers would catch AIDS and far more likely that they would catch herpes or gonorrhea. I didn't care either way. I can't count how many times I've been infected with the herpes virus. I've damn near got it everywhere," I said with a nervous chuckle.

"Want to know how many you gave me?" Tina asked.

Her eyes were full of pain and death. She lashed out with the straight razor, bisecting my bottom lip. I howled in anguish. She seized my hair and told me not to move as she brought the razor toward my eye. I thrashed my head back and forth, trying to free myself from her grasp.

"Hold still before you lose a fucking eye! I don't care either way. I can take your eyelid or your whole eye. It's up to you."

Pathetically, I began to cry. I know. Not very manly. When it comes down to it, I'm kind of a pussy. I've never been particularly strong. My sarcastic rapier wit and practiced stoicism were my primary weapons of self-defense. But my carefully cultivated affectation of calm aloofness disappeared at the thought of this mad whore carving my eye from my skull.

The cuts she'd already made on my face and chest had been tolerable. Syphilis and herpes had already ruined my once-handsome features. My nose had rotted off months ago, and my lips were so blistered and poxed they bore a greater resemblance to two pinkish sea anemones than anything that should have been on a face. Even my eyelids were encrusted with bunches of glistening red herpes ulcers. But this new horror made my asshole clench and my scrotum rise up tight against me. I was shivering in fear, blubbering nonsensical words, promises, and apologies.

"Please don't do this. I'm sorry. I'm so sorry. I didn't mean to get you sick. I didn't mean—I didn't. I'm sorry, okay? *I'm sorry! I'm sorry! nooooooo! Ahhhhhhhhhh! Stop! Stop!*"

She cut deep. The sharp blade traveled just below my eyebrow, slicing through skin, subcutaneous fat, and facial muscle, scraping my orbital bone. I tried not to move, positive she would make good on her threat to cut my eyeball out of my head if I resisted. I bit my cut lip, which had fallen to both sides of my mouth like open stage curtains. I screamed and cried as I watched her peel the severed scrap of flesh from my eye like the skin of a grape. My eye rolled around in its socket, seeking an escape from the duct tape that bound me to the chair, the locked room, the agony, my own skull.

"Shut the fuck up! Shut your bitch ass up before I cut off the other one!"

I complied, stifling my screams to pitiful whimpers like a scolded child.

Tina held the knife to my top lip. I noticed she was chewing something. She hadn't been chewing before, and I hadn't seen her open any food or bubblegum. I looked on the floor for my missing eyelid as the horrible revelation hit me that she'd most likely popped the herpes-riddled flesh right into her mouth and was now chewing it in my face while holding a knife to my lip, threatening to cut that off too. I wondered why she didn't hold it against my throat, but Tina knew I wasn't afraid of death. I was already dying from hepatitis, AIDS, syphilis, and at least two dozen other viruses and bacterial infections. She couldn't threaten me with that. She didn't want me dead. She wanted me in agony. She wanted me to watch her slowly unmake me cut by cut.

"How the fuck did you get so fucked up? Why would anyone want to catch diseases?"

I shrugged. "I don't knooooow," I whined, shaking my head as blood and tears continued to stream from my eyes and blur my vision. I couldn't even blink the blood and tears from my left eye with my eyelid gone.

"Yes you do. Oh, yes you do, and you're going to tell me all of it, or next, I'm cutting both your lips right off your ugly-ass face."

Tears, snot, blood, saliva, and fluids from the weeping sores and inflamed pustules leaked and slobbered down my face, hanging off my chin in long ropes.

"Okay. I'll tell you." All the torture wasn't necessary. I had every intention of telling her everything. I wasn't ashamed of any of it. In fact, I was proud.

"And don't be using a bunch of big ole fancy words. If I feel like I have to bust out a dictionary to understand your trick-ass, I'ma start cuttin' more shit off, you feel me? And you best not bore me either."

I nodded.

CHAPTER THREE

HORRIBLY INFECTED SEXUAL ORGANS

"My first sexual experience was being molested in the men's room at Woolworths," I began.

"If your ass is expecting sympathy from me, you can forget that shit! I was molested more times than I can count. I was only five years old the first time my pops made me suck his nasty old dick, and my mom's tricks was sticking it in me damn near every night by the time I was ten, and I ain't turn out like you!" Tina said, still holding the straight razor dangerously close to my face.

"It's not an excuse, just an explanation. It's important for you to hear the whole story if you really want to know why I turned out like this."

Tina nodded. "Okay, but if this shit starts to bore me, I'm cutting you again."

I swallowed hard and felt tears of cowardice return to my eyes, but I began talking anyway.

"Like I said, my first sexual experience was being molested in the men's room at Woolworth's…"

I was seven years old, and I had gone there with my mother so she could buy a new set of bath towels. She said I could pick out a toy if I was quiet and patient and didn't complain about how long it was taking her to shop. I remember she looked at dish towels, then pots and pans, sets of dishes and silverware, then we somehow ended up in the ladies' clothing section with her trying on dresses.

We'd been there for almost an hour and hadn't looked at bath towels yet, but I kept quiet because I really wanted a new Hot Wheels car. They had just come out with one that looked like the Mach 5 from Speed Racer, and I just had to have it. So I sat patiently while my mom looked through racks of skirts and dresses. Then I had to go to the bathroom. So I asked my mom, and she pointed to the men's room and went back to holding gaudy flower-print sundresses up to herself before draping them over her arms to take with her into the dressing room.

I had never gone to a public bathroom by myself. My dad had always gone with me, but Dad wasn't here and I was too old to go into the ladies' room with Mom. Besides, Mom was busy. So I went to the bathroom myself for the first time.

There was a man in the restroom when I walked in. He was standing by the sink washing his hands. He looked like a game show host. That's what I remember about him. He had nice hair, perfectly quaffed as if he was getting ready for a photo-shoot. His mustache curled up on the ends like handlebars, and he wore a sky-blue suit with wide lapels. I don't think I had ever seen anyone wear a suit that color before. There was almost something clownish about it. I remember him smiling at me, and I remember how wrong that smile looked. Even being that young, I knew adults weren't supposed to smile at kids that way. He smiled at me the way a man smiles at a pretty girl. I wanted to get away from that creepy smile as quickly as possible.

I rushed into the nearest stall, but before I could shut the door behind me, the game show host pushed his way into the stall with me. I was too young to understand the things he made me do. I remember crying, choking on his thick penis as he aggressively rammed it to the back of my throat while gripping my head in his massive hands. I remember his sweaty, hairy balls slapping my chin, and I remember the taste of his semen when it flooded my mouth and he forced me to swallow it. I remember him patting me on the head and telling me I had done a good job and then leaning down until he was eye level with me and warning me not to tell anyone. The man had a shiny silver revolver. He pulled it from his jacket and put the short barrel in my mouth where his cock had just been. I can still taste the cold metal. I remember wanting to kill that man, the impotent rage burning like bile in the back of my throat, but being so afraid I was completely paralyzed.

"Tell your mother and I'll shoot her dead right in this store. Tell your father and I'll shoot him in the face, but not before I tell him what a little sissy you are and how you begged me to let you suck my cock. Just imagine how disappointed he'll be when he finds out he raised a faggot."

That was the first time I'd been called that, but it certainly wasn't the last. The man tucked his pistol back in his waistband, took out a handkerchief, and wiped some semen off my chin that had dribbled out of my mouth. Then he checked himself in the mirror, ran a comb through his hair, straightened his collar, and walked out of the restroom and out of the store. I was so terrified I stood there for a long time before I realized I'd wet myself.

When I ran out of the restroom to find my mother, I didn't say anything to her about the game show host who'd molested me. I just asked her if she could buy me another pair of pants and some underwear. My mother was pissed, no pun intended, but not nearly as enraged as she would be two weeks later when a trip to the family physician revealed I'd contracted herpes. It had broken out on my lips and inside my mouth. I had no choice but tell my parents what happened. My father, just as the game show host had warned, called me several homosexual slurs and pretty much blamed me for the encounter. So that's how I got my first venereal disease. That's what they called it back then. VD.

Tina crossed her arms over her chest and waved the scalpel. "I still don't see how you get from gettin' throat-fucked in a bathroom to collectin' diseases and spreadin' 'em to my black ass!"

"Patience. I am getting to all that."

Her eyes flashed brilliant with rage, and she closed the space between us before I could blink. "Don't fucking tell me to be patient!"

This time she punched me. It was sudden and unexpected. Caught me right in the mouth and sent my two top front teeth flying. I had been slapped and beaten by past lovers before, both consensually and nonconsensually, but I couldn't recall ever being punched in the mouth. The pain was sharp and sudden, but milder than I would have expected. I felt a searing pain like fire in the space between my upper lip and where my nose would have been if not for the syphilis. She'd been holding the razor when she'd struck me and had cut me in addition to knocking out a couple teeth. The pain quickly receded to a dull ache. But I somehow felt humiliated by the way I'd been struck.

My swollen lip and missing teeth filled me with an odd sort of shame. There was something disrespectful about being punched in the mouth by a woman. I realized this was just my own misogyny speaking. I wouldn't feel the same if she had slapped me again or if she'd been a man. That was certainly not very enlightened of me, but I couldn't help the way I felt. I experienced a moment of profound outrage. How dare she! I was about to go full Karen on her before reminding myself of the power dynamics at play. I was her prisoner, and when compared to all I could and likely would endure at her hands, a few lost teeth and some humiliation was relatively minor.

"I was–I was just trying to get my thoughts in order. I'm sorry. I didn't mean to offend you."

Tina paced in front of me, glaring at me, nostrils flared and muscles flexed, taking deep, heavy breaths like a pugilist preparing themselves for the next round of brutality. Her eyes left me and traveled to the table where her torture devices were displayed and then down to the hand that still held the straight razor.

"No, please. I'm sorry. I was just trying to think," I whined, no longer as concerned about my dignity.

She stopped pacing and just stared at me with a furrowed brow and a scowl. The hand with the blood-caked razor began to rise, and I wept and shook in fear. Then she lowered her hand and shook her head, appearing to awaken from some murderous fugue and recognize my humanity, if only for a moment. It occurred to me how much easier it must be to dehumanize me now because of my monstrous appearance. It is much easier to show sympathy for the beautiful. Something within us seems almost hardwired to reward beauty and delight in punishing ugliness, as every preschool or kindergarten teacher on Earth could no doubt confirm. But sometimes, one's very hideousness could be a source of pity if not empathy. I thought I saw just a hint of pity in Tina's eyes for the hideous, pathetic creature blubbering and bleeding before her.

"Okay, motherfucker. You've had time to get yo' thoughts straight. So, fuckin' talk."

"I–I guess the fetish really took hold in junior high school. I guess they call it middle school now…" I began.

Back in middle school, our health teacher, Mister Giddleman—a tall, former college basketball player with a big curly red afro and what the kids today would call a "porn stache"—attempted to scare us all away from premarital sex by making us watch a forty-five-minute film about sexually transmitted infections. He wheeled out a cheap 8mm projector and a pop-up screen and set it up in front of the class before turning off the lights.

He didn't give us much warning about the content. He just said, "Watch this movie. There will be a few pop questions afterward."

Then he turned on the projector, grabbed his newspaper, and sat down at his desk with his feet propped up and his desk light on so he could read the sports pages while we were traumatized by images of diseased genitalia.

The film was just one endless collage of horribly infected sexual organs, dripping, oozing, and bleeding, with a narrator describing the symptoms in morbid detail. Graphic films like these were not entirely new to us. We'd watched one the month before warning of the dangers of playing on railroad tracks that had shown people with amputated limbs, closed casket funerals, iron rails that glistened with blood and viscera, ending with a shot of a mannequin on the tracks being decimated by a locomotive doing eighty miles an hour.

Prior to that, we were treated to a film about heroin addicts, PCP, cocaine, and amphetamine users that featured a woman going through withdrawals, sweating, writhing, moaning, screaming, and vomiting in a barren room that looked like an attic and had only a blood- and piss-stained mattress on the floor. There were testimonials from policemen who'd scraped bodies off the pavement of drug addicts who thought they could fly and leapt from buildings. And one of a woman who'd fried her own infant in a pan. The message was clear—don't do drugs or this could be you.

Even back in elementary school they showed us films of kids getting run over by cars to warn us to look both ways before crossing the street, cross in the crosswalk, and obey the streetlights and traffic signs. The '80s were a different time. Films like those wouldn't fly in today's touchy-feely world, but they were common in the seventies and eighties. But this one—this one was by far the worst.

Ghastly images of inflamed vaginas covered in suppurating sores like some venomous sea creature paraded across the screen to our astonishment and amusement. There were as many chuckles and snickers as there were groans and gasps. Our pubescent brains were not quite mature enough to absorb the message they were attempting to convey in the manner they were trying to convey it. It was just too much. It seemed unreal. Testicles swollen to the size of grapefruits. Gangrenous penises rotting like overripe bananas and dripping a rainbow of unctuous fluids that you could almost smell through the screen. Labia so riddled with herpes they looked like fried pork rinds coated in hot sauce. For many of us, these films were the only genitalia we'd ever seen besides our own. There was no internet back then. Even as I groaned in disgust and tried to look away, I couldn't help the stiffening of my own sex, hardened by a tsunami of pubescent hormones. Confused by images both revolting and arousing. It was like watching the worst horror movie and the most graphic porn flick combined into one insane cinematic experience.

That same day, while walking home from school, I found myself stroking a painful erection through the hole in my pocket, playing the images in my head over and over again. I went home and masturbated furiously and for the very first time. I had my very first orgasm. It was so unexpected I thought I'd broken something. I honestly didn't know what was happening. But it felt so good I masturbated four more times that evening.

The next morning, my penis was chafed raw and swollen up like a yam. Not knowing everything about STIs at that age, I worried I'd given myself one through masturbation. I was concerned, not about my own health and safety but about my parents finding out what I'd done. So I told no one. Of course, in a day or two, it went back to normal. Once everything down there was normal, I promptly flagellated myself again, beating my cock like an undisciplined child. And do you know what I thought about every time I masturbated? Do you know what images filled my mind? The game show host's lice-ridden pubic hair, the putrid stench of the infection issuing from his swollen glans, and the herpes sores sprouting like pomegranate seeds up and down the base of his cock.

The funny thing is I'm not even certain that's actually what his cock looked like. I can clearly remember that big purple knob as it was being aimed at my face, but I suspect the rest of the imagery came from those films Mister Giddleman showed us in health class. Certainly, my molester did have herpes, but I don't know if it was in full bloom the way it was in my imagination. And my assailant's penis wasn't the only thing I fantasized about. I imagined rancid vaginas and cantaloupe-sized testicles. I imagined pox-filled mouths and ulcerous tongues that looked like mine when I had an outbreak. I imagined gaping reddened anuses circled with halos of bleeding red bumps and purulent blisters. I fantasized about sticking my cock in them all to defile myself, fucking that sewer of pestilence and corruption, stirring it into a frothy stew with my young cock. Every horror Mister Giddleman had shown my class to dissuade us from promiscuity had now become the very inspiration for it in my mind. I longed to sample that smorgasbord of infection and disease. I wanted to bathe in that river of pus, semen, vaginal fluid, discharge, and liquid rot. It wasn't long before I was frequenting park bathrooms and alleyways. By the time I was in high school, I had been used in every way a young male body could conceivably be used.

"Okay, so that's why you did it? That's how you developed this little kink? Because your gym teacher showed you some nasty videos?" Tina said, turning on a butane torch and approaching me with it. "I'm actually happy. I was worried you were going to say something to make me feel sorry for what I'm about to do to your ass."

She knelt between my legs and turned the flame of the torch on the remains of the testicle she'd ruptured. The pain defied every description I am capable of. It was like sitting on a barbecue with my nuts hanging onto the coals. I smelled my own flesh cooking, a sweet, smoky stench that would have been delicious were it not my own savaged meat being cooked. My screams would have been the envy of Prince and Freddy Mercury. At some point, I lost consciousness.

CHAPTER FOUR

THE SALTY, SEMISWEET TASTE OF HER CUM

THEY SAY THAT DREAMS ARE WHEN YOUR MIND LOSES THE TIGHT grip it holds on sanity when you are awake and allows itself to relax and go insane. My dreams were of demons and cherubs fucking in pools of blood, vomit, and excrement on the floor of a truck stop bathroom. In the dream, I was reciting the Lord's Prayer while being sodomized by a devil with muscles like a bodybuilder and a cock like a porn star while he raked fiery claws down the shaft of my cock, shredding my penis and scrotum while simultaneously cauterizing them. I screamed in agony and ejaculated in ecstasy and then woke to Tina standing above me. She had the straight razor in her hand again.

"I want to hear the rest of it. I want you to tell me about everyone you fucked. Every motherfucker you gave this shit to and every motherfucker who gave it to you, and I want names. Especially the motherfuckers who got you sick."

"Why? Are you going to hunt them down and kill them too?"

"Maybe. Depends on what you tell me. But don't go

changin' the story up to protect 'em. If I even think you're lyin' to me, I'm gonna take an apple peeler to your cock. You get me?"

"Yes. Yes, I get you. I'll tell you everything."

Tina looked over at where she'd laid out various torture implements, most of which looked like they came from her kitchen and garage. She was looking at the apple peeler. I could almost see her mind churning. I imagined she was thinking the same thing I was: *How do you skin a limp dick?*

I was hoping neither of us would find out. "Where do you want me to begin?"

"You said you started hanging out in park bathrooms and bars. Is that where you got these diseases?"

I nodded. "Yes. Some of them. I made a hole in a bathroom stall in the park. A glory hole. I put duct tape around it to cover the sharp edges so no one would cut themselves when they shoved their dick through. I would go there after school and just sit and wait."

"And how old were you?"

"I was in high school. I guess it started my freshman year."

"And you never got to see what nasty perverts shoved their dicks through that hole?"

I shook my head and instantly regretted it. True to her word, Tina could tell I was lying. She grabbed the apple peeler.

"Wait-wait-wait-wait! Okay, there were a few I met. Some guys would wait around to see who stepped out of the opposite stall. I usually stayed put until they left. Some guys were probably hoping there was a girl in there, and I didn't want to find myself in any kind of physical altercation with a homophobe. But sometimes, they would speak to me, and I could tell by their voices they knew I was a boy."

Tina still held the apple peeler, glaring murderously at me as she searched my face for any hint of deception.

"Once, I came out of the stall because I heard a voice that

almost sounded female in its timbre and melody. Do you understand? It wasn't just the higher pitch, but it had that singsong quality to it that many women have. I was confused because I had just had this person's dick in my mouth. The salty, semisweet taste of her cum still lay thick on my tongue. She was standing just outside the stall door, and I heard that lyrical voice ask, 'Who are you? I want to meet you.' So I looked out…"

The woman standing in that filthy public bathroom was a head taller than me, with long, dyed blue and red hair. She wore torn black fishnet stockings and a black spandex miniskirt that hugged her narrow hips and slender thighs. A black lace shirt with a black bra beneath it covered her chest, and her lips, nails, and eyeshadow were all raven black. I had never heard the term transgender before, but I knew this was a different creature than any I had so far encountered. She was otherworldly, a beautiful goth woman with a long, thick cock, eyes like a wolf, and a voice like an angel. I fell in love at the sight of her.

"How old are you? You're just a child," the woman said.

I was barely fifteen, but I didn't want to scare her away, so I lied.

"I'm nineteen. How old are you?" I asked, still transfixed by this enigmatic beauty.

"I'm twenty-two. What's your name? What are you doing giving blowjobs to strangers in a bathroom?"

"Joey," I replied, answering one question but not the other.

"I'm Esmerelda. Do you have a home, Joey?"

I was still living in my parents' house, but it hadn't felt like a home since that day in the bathroom at Woolworth's.

"No," I replied.

"Would you like to come home with me?" Esmeralda asked, and I wanted nothing more on this earth in that moment.

"And what did you catch from her? Did you tell her you had

herpes and whatever else you got sucking all those cocks?" Tina asked.

"I would think, from one cocksucker to another, you would be a little less judgmental," I said, then instantly regretted it. I needed to get a tighter rein upon my sarcasm.

Tina stepped close, pointing with the straight razor like it was a mere extension of her finger. "I ain't no slut. I'm a whore. There's a difference. I suck dick because that's how I pay my bills. I ain't doin' it because I like the taste, or because I like having a gallon of cum sloshing around in my belly every night, or to catch some motherfucker's funky-ass disease!"

My scrotum was still on fire. I was shivering all over. My body was losing heat through the damaged tissue, and my temperature was plummeting. I was probably also going into shock. The damage she'd done to my manhood was catastrophic. Even my cock and remaining testicle had been charred. If I hadn't been before, I was now utterly terrified of Tina. Terrified of all the horrible implements she'd brought along with her. Terrified of her seemingly limitless capacity for cruelty. "No. You're right. I apologize. It is different. And to answer your question, all I got from her was crabs and genital warts. Nothing too severe."

"And what did you give her? Did she catch herpes from you?"

"Yes, but don't weep for her too much. Esmeralda was not exactly a hapless victim. If anything, I was her victim. Or rather, we victimized each other. Remember, I was still just a kid."

"Fuck that! You knew what you were doing!"

I winced at her angry words, bracing for another attack. But once again, I was able to cool her down by nodding in agreement with her. "I did. I did know what I was doing. You're right. I was a kid trying to live out my fantasies and experience everything, and I was selfish and irresponsible."

"Damn right you were!" Tina replied, still waving the straight razor.

"I stayed with Esmeralda for three years. It turned out she was a sex worker, and she showed me how to make money turning tricks. Esmeralda was incredibly intelligent—one of the smartest people I knew. She turned tricks at night and went to college during the day. She was working on a master's degree in psychology. She encouraged me to go back to school and get my GED and then helped me fill out my college applications. If it hadn't been for her, I'm sure I would have died on the streets."

Tina scoffed. "That would'n've been no damn great tragedy. At least then I wouldn't have met your twisted ass."

I nodded my agreement.

"Okay, so where's Esmeralda now? Why ain't y'all still together?"

For the first time during our encounter, I began to weep from emotional pain rather than physical torture.

"She was murdered. Some evil trick tore her apart. They said it was a hate crime. Someone thought they were getting a natural-born woman, assigned female at birth, and perhaps only found out she was trans while consummating their transaction. Some guys have such fragile masculinity they can't handle the idea of any sexual fulfillment from anyone but a biological woman."

Tina's angry mask appeared to soften just a bit. "Yeah. I run into those types too, and I'm all natural. They start off all sweet and loving until they cum, then they get violent 'cause they disgusted with themselves for fuckin' a whore. I imagine it's even worse for a transwoman. So what did you do then?"

"I fulfilled Esmeralda's wishes, her dreams for me. I got my degree, got a real job writing computer code."

"But you kept chasing diseases?"

I looked Tina directly in the face with my one good eye. "I

tried to stop. I even went to meetings for sex and love addicts, but that just gave me a new hunting ground."

CHAPTER FIVE

AS MY BOWELS WERE PUMMELED BY TWO HUGE COCKS

It was at Sex Addicts Anonymous that I learned there was a name for people like me—bug catchers. I had never heard the term before, and rather than feeling like an insult or something to be ashamed of, it felt good to put a label on my odd little kink. The meetings were held in the basement of an old Baptist church downtown. The pastor was a grizzled old Black man who'd once been a singer in a popular R&B group in the seventies. He had kind eyes that beamed like headlights from a face that looked like black leather. His grey hair was pulled back into a ponytail, and I never saw that man without a tie on. I was surprised to see someone like him leading the SAA meetings and felt a little self-conscious. Usually, these types of meetings are run by other addicts. You don't have a teetotaler running an Alcoholics Anonymous meeting.

He began the meeting by telling his own story.

"I cheated on my wife damn near a hundred times. I loved her more than anything, but I never met a stripper I didn't love just as much. It got so I was going to strip clubs every night. If I couldn't convince one of them to jack me off or suck me off in the Champagne room for an extra hundred dollars, I would ring up my favorite call girl. My wife didn't deserve that. She was a good woman, but I just couldn't help myself."

I nodded, thinking about Esmeralda. I had loved her too, but I still couldn't resist my fetish for diseases. No matter how many times she made me promise to use a condom when I went on a date with a client, I just couldn't bring myself to do it. Nothing made me harder than that rotten egg aroma of infection from a leaking penis or vagina. The instant I smelled it, I wanted it in my mouth. I wanted to consume it, to suck the disease right out of them. Esmeralda would be furious with me, but she would always forgive me.

They went around the room, and everyone had a chance to tell their story. One man was addicted to porn and masturbated a dozen times a day. There was a white suburban woman who was addicted to sex with strange Black men. She would rent hotel rooms and arrange BBC gangbangs with men she met on the internet. A couple others were addicted to prostitutes, and one was just a playa, a self-proclaimed ladies' man who fucked five or six women a day. Finally, it was my turn to speak.

"I have a fetish for sexually transmitted diseases. I collect them. I have sex with women, men, young, old, it doesn't matter. I just look for the ones who look the sickest. I don't care about their sex or gender; it's the prospect of contracting another infection that attracts me."

"You're a bug catcher," Pastor John said.

"A what?"

"A bug catcher. Someone who deliberately gets themselves infected with HIV. We had one in here a year and half or two years ago. He wound up dying of AIDS."

"Bug catcher," I whispered, turning the words over on my tongue and rolling them around in my mouth to examine them from all sides. I liked it. It suited me.

I kept going to those meetings, but they didn't help because

I didn't want to be helped. I was only going to make Esmeralda happy. As soon as she died, I just stopped going. By then, I had already fucked half the regular attendees, including the pastor himself.

"The pastor? You fucked the damn pastor?" The surprise on her face gave way to a small chuckle. "Boy, you somethin' else, ain't you?"

I couldn't help feeling a bit of pride. My conquests were more about the diseases than the people, but I would be lying if I didn't say I took some joy in how I always found a way to get who and what I wanted sexually.

"Yeah, I fucked the pastor, or rather, he fucked me."

The meeting that night was charged with even more sexual energy than usual. There was a new woman there that evening. A thick-thighed, wide-bottomed, middle-aged woman with shockingly red hair, named Samantha. When it was Samantha's turn to speak, she told a story about having an anal threesome with two bisexual men, one sandwiched in the middle so he was penetrating her while being penetrated from behind. It wasn't so much the story she told but how she told it. It was like I was reading hardcore erotica.

She described the feeling of the man penetrating her well-lubed anus and how she could feel his cock swell each time the other man thrust into him from behind. At one point, they were synced up so that the man who was fucking the guy fucking her would thrust forward, and she imagined his cock was going through the man between them directly into her. It ended with them double-penetrating her, but not like you would think. Not a dick in her vagina and one in her asshole. She had two cocks in her ass at once.

While she was describing the scene, I found myself getting aroused. I never wore underwear, so my reaction to her story was obvious to anyone who was looking, and someone was. Two someones had taken notice of me: the pastor and a punk rock kid in his mid-twenties with a big platinum mohawk who wore a leather jacket with no shirt and had a six-pack more from lack of nutrients than exercise. He had a sensuous mouth, full lips that sort of pouted. His mouth reminded me of Mick Jagger, but his face was more Pee Wee Herman. His eyes locked on to mine, and slowly and deliberately trailed their way down to my crotch and back up to my eyes again. No more needed to be said. We were both sex addicts. We'd done this dance many times before. We knew what the signals meant.

I turned to look at the pastor, who was giving me the same look. Only this time, it was I who let my eyes wander and was surprised to see that he, too, was building a tent in his pants. Things were getting interesting.

"Don't tell me you fucked both of 'em?" Tina asked, appearing not just intrigued by my story but stimulated by it. She reached down under her miniskirt and began rubbing her swollen clit. "Tell me what happened," she implored me.

"The meeting ended, and Punk Pee Wee and I stayed behind to help the pastor clean up. Once everyone else was gone, I walked over and locked the door and just started undressing."

"Just like that? You didn't say anything to them?"

I shrugged. "What was I supposed to say? We all knew what was about to happen. The only question was who was going to be on the bottom and who was going to be on top, and I answered that by taking position on my knees. The pastor dropped his pants, and pretty soon, I had a long, thick Black cock in my throat and an equally long cock in my ass. I enjoyed it, but it wasn't the same as fucking someone I knew was carrying an STI. Punk Pee Wee certainly looked the part of a disease carrier, but I thought it would be rude to ask. Then the pastor got an idea..."

"Why don't we try what Samantha was talking about? What she did with those two guys?"

Punk Pee Wee smiled sadistically. "Two in one hole?"

The pastor nodded. Something about his smile reminded me of an evil Bill Cosby. "Yeah, two in one hole."

Clearly, I'm not vanilla, but I was never really into pain. I didn't go to BDSM parties or enjoy being tied up and spanked. Whips and chains were never my thing. I have been urinated on, defecated on, vomited on, and covered in semen nearly from head to toe. I have called men Daddy and women Mommy and role-played everything from a toddler to a French maid, but getting fucked in the ass by two well-endowed men was a very new and excruciating prospect. I considered refusing, even opened my mouth to protest, but they didn't wait for my consent. When I struggled, the pastor held me down. Punk Pee Wee squirted more lube into my already dilated rectum and began easing his fingers inside me. First two, then three, then four, then his entire fist. I wept and squealed but lost the ability to form words. I just went completely numb. I dissociated from my body and just lay there on the church floor and let them use me. When the punk kid removed his fist and replaced it with his cock, the pastor came and joined him. It was like I was somewhere outside myself. It felt like I was watching it all on a video monitor as my bowels were pummeled by two huge cocks.

Tina nodded. "Yeah, I know that feeling. I learned all about that when my mom's tricks started adding me to the evenin' menu. It's a trauma response. You got raped is what happened." Her voice sounded almost sympathetic. She let out a sigh and fell silent.

I nodded. She was right. I looked up at her, but my eyes were so caked in blood I couldn't see much of her expression. All I could tell was that she wasn't masturbating anymore.

CHAPTER SIX
SEEING MY OWN FLESH SLOWLY EXCISED...

I WAS EIGHTEEN BEFORE I HAD SEX WITH A BIOLOGICAL WOMAN for the first time. It was my first year in college. Her name was Beth and she was rumored to be the most promiscuous girl on the campus. But compared to what I had become accustomed to at that point, she was practically virginal. She was the closest I'd ever come to normal sex with a regular person.

We met at a sorority house party. I was feeling pretty good about myself that night. I hadn't had a herpes breakout in months, and even though I think I already had gonorrhea, chlamydia, and syphilis, it wasn't smelling or looking too poorly down there yet. So I took a shot.

I grabbed a couple drinks and sat next to her, offering her one.

"Thanks. There's no GHB or anything in this is there?"

She could tell by the confusion on my face that I had no idea what she was asking me. "I–I don't know. I didn't read the label."

Beth let out the loudest ear-splitting laugh I'd ever heard. "You're cute. What's your name?"

"You're cute too. What's your name?" I replied.

She drunkenly slurred some name that began with a B that I didn't quite hear over the loud music and loud voices, but it felt like too much effort to ask her to repeat it. I didn't bother telling her my name either. I couldn't imagine she would have actually cared.

"Want to hear something funny?" I asked.

She took a sip of the drink I'd given her, though sip is probably too passive a word for the big gulp she took. Then she smiled at me.

"Yes. Tell me something funny."

"I've never performed cunnilingus."

"Cunning-cunning what?"

"Oral sex. I've never performed oral sex on a woman. I've never licked a vagina."

Her eyes widened in surprise, and she almost appeared sober for a moment. "You've never eaten pussy?"

I have always despised vulgar colloquialisms like eating pussy. When you eat something, you don't leave it intact. It is consumed. It becomes nourishment, sustenance. I had no desire to cannibalize a woman's vagina. I just wanted to experience the act of pleasuring one.

I shook my head. "No. Never."

She gave me a sly wink and a drunken smile. "Sooooooo, you wanna lick my pussy?"

I returned her smile. "Very much so."

The party was at a sorority house, one of which she was a member. She knocked back the rest of her drink in one gulp like a dockworker at the end of a grueling shift, seized my hand, and led me up the stairs to her room. The door had not fully shut behind me before she was shimmying her flat ass and narrow hips out of her Daisy Dukes and falling backward onto the bed with her legs spread wide.

The silken pink folds of her vagina were like the petals of a flower moist with morning dew. It was the first vagina I had ever seen in person. I had expected it to look like the hairy, suppurating maws in Mister Giddleman's sex education films, but this one was neatly shaved and appeared clean and healthy. You can't imagine how disappointed I was.

I lay on my belly like a sniper and gathered Beth's smooth thighs in my arms. I took a deep whiff of her. It wasn't the heavy animal funk I was used to from men. She smelled of blood, urine, and old seafood, floral soaps, and perfumed lotions, and tasted both tart and bitter, sweet and salty, like semen, goat cheese, and lime juice. I found the little nub between the folds of her labia and circled it with my tongue as I sucked it, treating it like a very small, underdeveloped cock. She seized my head in both hands and smashed her vagina against my face, bruising my upper lip with her pelvic bone. My tongue was still pressed to her clit, only the pressure of her thrusting hips was so powerful I couldn't move it. She ground her clitoris against my tongue like a pestle grinding spices in a mortar, pressing my tongue hard against my own teeth and making me fear it would be severed or at the very least gashed and torn into a useless lump as I tasted trickles of my own blood.

When she came, it was like she had turned feral. She banged her vagina against my mouth, busting my lip and further cutting my tongue against my teeth. Her grip on the sides of my head intensified. The college girl's manicured nails dug into my scalp and temples like the talons of a falcon snatching prey. My own sex responded to both the pain and her convulsing orgasms, and I found myself cumming too. Hot semen filled my boxers, plastering them to my thighs. I lifted my head from between her thighs and could barely catch my breath.

"Wow! You sure that was your first time?" she asked. "Because you've got talent! You ever eat ass before?"

Of course I had. I had licked Esmeralda's little brown rosebud many times, but I had never done that to a woman who had been assigned female at birth. For some reason, I felt like she'd be disappointed if she knew hers was not the first anus I'd tongued, so I didn't answer, I just gently flipped her over onto her stomach and slid my tongue between her tight little ass cheeks.

"Oh, fuck this! Why the fuck you think I want to hear some story about you licking some bitch's stank ass? You just stallin'!"

She pinched my nipple. Not playfully or seductively, but gripping it between her thumb and pointer finger along with three or four inches of skin, fat, and pectoral muscle and twisted it hard, like a grandmother disciplining a fidgeting child in church. It hurt, but not remarkably so when compared to taking a torch to my testicles or cutting off my eyelid. But then I saw the glint of steel in her other hand as she brought the straight razor to my chest. Still holding my nipple like a vice, she began sawing at my pectoral muscle, cutting deep, separating pectoralis major from pectoralis minor. The blade bounced over my ribcage like a xylophone as she removed my chest muscle like she was fileting a fish.

"Ahhh! Noooo! Noooo! Stop, stop, stop, Staaaaaaaaahp!"

The razor went back into her pocket after doing a pretty good job of cutting my chest to the bone. Her long fingernails dug beneath the muscle and began to pull. I didn't believe any pain could rival the agony in my charred and ruptured scrotum. I was pretty confident she'd fucked up by going so extreme with the torture so soon and that nothing would seem too terrible after that. I was wrong. This agony very nearly rivaled it. Tina's stiletto heel lancing my diseased testicle had been quick. Even the torch she'd used on it had only been there a few seconds. It was the lingering agony afterward that had been the most intense. But this wrenching and jerking on my chest, trying to rip it off the bone, was a slow and terrible ordeal.

I was watching it happen, helpless to intervene and save myself. Seeing my own flesh slowly excised was almost as horrible as the pain. There's a famous scene in the original Hellraiser movie where Pinhead says to the young hero, "Your suffering will be legendary, even in hell." Watching her tug on my carved muscle, putting her foot on the right side of my chest for leverage while she slowly ripped my left chest muscle off the bone, I could not imagine hell contained many torments worse than those I was suffering at the hands of this insane woman. Second only to the intense agony was that nauseating wet tearing sound like duct tape being peeled off skin. When she was done removing the muscle, I could see movement behind my ribcage and realized I was witnessing the rhythmic thump of my own heart. Once again, darkness rushed in to save me from the pain and horror.

CHAPTER SEVEN

THICK DOLLOPS OF COAGULATED SEMEN AND VAGINAL YEAST ...

Tina was staring at me when I woke up.

"Okay, I want to hear the rest of the story."

I shook my head, blubbering and crying like a smacked toddler. "No! You're just going to keep hurting me!"

Tina grabbed me by my jaw and forced me to meet her furious gaze. "You can be damn sure I will if you don't talk to me. At least if you keep me entertained, you can delay it a while. Ya might even tell me something that makes me take pity on your sick, twisted ass. Otherwise, I got shit over on that table I ain't even decided how I want to use yet. If you don't want me to start gettin' creative, you better keep me interested, motherfucker!"

She shoved my face away so hard the chair went up on two legs, and for a moment, I feared it would topple over. But gravity pulled the chair back into place. I looked at the beautiful raging street whore and thought about what she'd said.

It made sense; maybe if I talked long enough, kept her distracted, someone would find me, rescue me, or I could figure out some way to save myself.

"So she wanted me to lick her asshole, so that's what I did…"

I tongued her little brown rosebud while Beth masturbated to one climax after another as my tongue explored her rectum, licking her clean from the inside. Soon, we were hooking up almost every night. I wasn't the only guy she was having sexual relations with. Sometimes, I could taste other men on her. One day she came into my dorm room all sweaty, makeup smeared, hair a mess, and told me she needed to take a shower because she'd just had an orgy with six dudes from the basketball team.

"That's not an orgy. That's a gangbang. An orgy would involve more than just one woman, unless the guys were fucking each other too. If they were all just fucking you, that's a gangbang."

She looked at me, cocked her head, and smiled. "Is someone jealous?"

I suppose most men would have been jealous, but I have never been built that way. I wasn't jealous. I was turned on.

"Did you use a condom?" I asked.

She looked away sheepishly and replied, "No, I didn't."

"Did they ejaculate inside you?"

This time she just nodded, still looking away.

"Where?"

"What do you mean, where?" she asked, turning to look at me with a raised eyebrow.

"Did they ejaculate in your mouth? In your vagina? In your anus? Where?"

"All–all three, I-I guess," she stammered.

"And you haven't showered yet?"

She shook her head slowly, hesitantly, still not certain where I was going with my questions. That surprised me. I thought she knew me better than that.

"Come here. Take off your clothes."

"I really need to shower first. I've still got cum all up inside me."

"Good," I replied, taking her arm and pulling her over to my bed.

I began ripping off her clothes, popping the buttons on her shorts in my eagerness to get to her. As soon as I slid down her sticky pink underwear and saw the glistening slick custard of curdled semen and vaginal fluids, a malodorous greenish yellow discharge I was certain was infected with trichomoniasis, I licked it from the fabric greedily, shuddering with excitement to consume the rot within her.

Her eyes widened. Revulsion contorted her features, but her disgust quickly turned to rapture as I slid my tongue inside her, searching for the rest of the semen and whatever diseases it might contain. Thick dollops of coagulated semen and vaginal yeast fell onto my outstretched tongue. I swallowed this fetid pudding of pestilence, choking it down with a satisfied grin, then turned my attention to the glistening brown ring of her asshole. It looked like she was shitting cake batter. Diarrhea, blood, lubricant, and the sperm of a half dozen young jocks leaked from her torn rectum like frosting from a cake decorating tube. They had been rough with her here, tearing her tissue in their eagerness to mine their own pleasure from her flesh. I could taste her blood and fecal discharge in addition to the cocktail of jock semen. I licked her clean, imbibing shit-streaked semen and blood as it leaked from her bowels, greedily consuming it all. I imagined I could taste chlamydia and syphilis, HPV, and genital warts in the mélange of oily, tangy fluids washing over my tongue.

Beth shuddered and convulsed with orgasm after screaming, cussing, hissing orgasm. I rose from between her legs and lay beside her. I was so aroused at that point that a few quick strokes were all it took to bring me to my own climax. She returned the favor by licking my seed from my belly.

"Okay, now you want to tell me what the fuck that was all about? You just licked my pussy better than you ever have after I told you I'd just been gangbanged by half the basketball team. What's up with that?"

That's when I told her about my fetish. After that, she would always come to me after having sex with other men, and it became my job to clean her up.

Tina stared at me in slack-jawed amazement and nodded. "I met a lot of tricks who want to go down on me before I clean up. They like the idea that other men have been inside me. Makes it dirtier, I guess. Some of 'em have cuckold fetishes they too afraid to tell they wives about, so they act 'em out with me. I had one who wanted me to call him whenever a condom broke, or after I fucked my pimp, so he could fuck me in their cum or lick it out of me."

She stared at me with an unreadable expression, and I realized she was talking about me. That's when I finally placed her. She was one of three prostitutes I used to use for that purpose when I was fresh out of college and working my first real job.

I was working in the financial district in Las Vegas for a Japanese import/export company that bought American products and made them available in Japan and vice versa. I was their computer guy, and I was making more money than I'd ever dreamed of, so of course I spent it on prostitutes.

"At first, I sought out the prettiest ones—like you. That lasted about a year. Then, as my hunger for more and more diseases grew insatiable, I began to seek out the worst, most addicted, worn out, and diseased whores I could find. It was during this time that I contracted the most virulent diseases."

There was one prostitute in particular, a crack- and meth-addicted old whore who could have been my mother's age. She had thin, flabby breasts striated with blue veins that hung down to her concave belly like empty bladders. Her legs were long and skinny with loose wrinkled skin hanging like gooseflesh from her thighs. A roadmap of varicose veins wound their way up from her calves to her crotch like a tangle of interconnected city streets. She was always unwashed, and whatever stew of noxious infections festered between her thighs remained untreated. She would call me up every morning, after a long night of turning fifty-dollar tricks at truck stops and bus stations, and I would rush to fuck her or lick her ass or her pussy, stirring that frothing cauldron of disease with my tongue or my cock, consuming a smorgasbord of rot and decay. She was the source of more than half the diseases I contracted. We traded viruses like baseball cards.

Tina's scowl of disgust twisted into something terrifying. I could see the struggle to hold at bay whatever violence fought to escape her. I knew it wouldn't be long before that fury broke free of its fetters and vented itself all over me.

"Let me stop you right fucking there. It's my turn."

I was confused. At first, I thought she meant to hurt me again, but then I realized she wanted to tell her story. But that wasn't all she wanted.

Tina kicked me in the chest, and the chair I was strapped to fell backward, landing with a crash on the hard concrete floor. I was still dazed when I saw Tina's hairless brown slit descending toward my face, blistered with an outbreak of herpes and leaking curds of thick yellow discharge tinged pink with menstrual blood. The smell was like a dumpster at a seafood restaurant, rotting shellfish and molding cheese. It made my eyes water and my stomach roil.

She straddled my face, thrusting her swollen vulva against my one remaining lip, pinning my tongue against my exposed teeth, and drawing blood as she humped my mouth, not waiting for me to participate, just grinding into me, using my lip and tongue like inanimate sex toys, crushing her diseased snatch against my bleeding mouth.

"Lick my pussy! Lick it like you used to!"

I did my best to comply, not wanting to anger her further. The cluster of raw blisters and sores around my mouth rubbed against the blisters on her labia, scraping them raw and reopening ones that had healed, popping the angry red pustules like zits, and leaking pus and blood into my mouth. It was a familiar taste, plague and infection. A delicacy I had sought out for years in one pestilent crotch after another. I began licking furiously at that virulent pit of rot and pox, seeking out her clitoris with my tongue to hasten her orgasm and free me from the prison of her thighs. The harder and faster I licked, the more aggressively she fucked my face with her dripping snatch, smearing a rank panty pudding across my lips and chin, banging my head against the concrete floor with each thrust of her pelvis, smothering me with her sex, drowning me in a tidal wave of pestilence. I choked and gagged, struggling for air, panicking at the possibility of being asphyxiated by this mad whore's rancid vagina.

Finally, Tina began to moan and shudder. Her legs trembled, her back arched, and her loins let loose a torrent of fluid I was pretty certain was mostly urine. I gagged and choked as it filled my throat, wondering if this had been her intention all along, to murder me with piss and vaginal fluid, drown me alive in female ejaculate. A fitting punishment for the man who'd used sex to rob her of her life.

Just when I was certain of my eminent death and had accepted my fate, Tina stood, allowing me to breathe. I gasped and coughed, sucking in great lungsful of air and spitting out piss and cum. The salty, vinegary taste of her discharge lingered on my tongue, warm and familiar, like being reunited with an old toxic friend.

Tina struggled to bring her own breathing back under control. "You always were good at licking pussy. I remember that about you. You were the only john I ever had who could always make me cum, every damn time. I'd tell you about the men I'd fucked that day, and you'd just go to town down there. It was the craziest, sexiest thing I'd ever seen. You were handsome then. Fine as hell, truthfully. Now your ass looks like death on a hot grill."

After finally getting my breathing under control, I risked asking a question. "If I'm so ugly now, why did you just do that?"

Tina laughed. There was little mirth in the sound. "Ain't no 'if' about it, fool. You're ugly as fuck now. Even before I cut off your lip and your eyelid, the herpes and syphilis had already fucked your face up. Talkin' about 'if,' nigga, your nose has rotted right the fuck off! Your lips and eyelids had so many herpes blisters on them it looked like you got stung by a swarm of bees. Ain't no fuckin' 'if' about that shit. You an ugly motherfucker now. Still, you always could make me cum better'n anyone else. Not even my pimp could get me off like you can. Until I seen how ugly you was now, I had even thought about just kidnapping you and keepin' you as a sex slave, but I can't look at that disgusting shit you call a face every day, and your dick looks even worse. That shit would give me nightmares. But I figured you already gave me the worst disease a whore could get. Fucked me up real good. It don't matter now what else I catch. Maybe I'll become a bug catcher too, huh?" Tina laughed again. It was a sad and evil sound that somehow made the room, already devoid of any semblance of happiness, even more joyless.

"Why are you doing all of this, Tina?"

"I already told your ass. I just wanted to get off."

I shook my head. "No, not why did you just grind your vagina into my face and almost smother me to death. I mean why are you doing all of this? Why did you track me down? Why did you kidnap me? Why are you torturing me?"

Tina's smile resembled the snarl of a predator before attacking a rival. I braced for more of her fury, as futile as that would be. Whatever violence she doled out next, I knew there would be no way to prepare for it.

Tina stood up my chair. Even with all the weight I had lost to my myriad illnesses, she still struggled to lift me upright, huffing and straining with the effort. Once I was settled in place once more, she picked up the straight razor again and began sawing off my other nipple as I screamed and screamed futilely. Then she turned her attention to my one remaining ear, my lip, and was considering my other eyelid when her eyes fell upon my dick. I knew this moment was coming, but I had been expecting to be simply castrated, a horrifying enough proposition. What she had in mind was far worse.

"Ever hear of a writer named Monica J. O'Rourke?"

I was exhausted from screaming, overwhelmed by pain, barely holding on to consciousness, but I knew I had better answer. What she might do to me if I didn't answer was unfathomable. I shook my head.

"No? *Suffer The Flesh*? *What Happens in the Darkness*? *In the End, Only Darkness*? *Poisoning Eros*? No? Too bad. She's sick as fuck. I mean she writes really twisted shit. I think a perverted fuck like you would appreciate her shit. But your conceited, saditty ass probably only reads French poetry or some shit, huh?"

I was in so much pain I couldn't formulate a response. I couldn't make any sense of what she was saying to me. I just shook my head again.

"Anyway, I love her shit. I used to read her books all the time. Reading that fucked-up shit helped me forget about my own fucked-up shit, you know? No matter how bad my night was—gettin' raped and robbed by a client, my pimp kickin' my ass—it was better than gettin' raped and tortured by demons in hell or by a bunch of sick fucks at a sadistic fat camp. You know what I'm sayin'?"

I shook my head. I had no idea what she was saying.

Tina rolled her eyes in exasperation. "Anyway, one of my favorite stories by her is called 'An Experiment in Human Nature.' I guess I'm glad you haven't read it; that way, this next part will be a surprise for your ass."

Tina left my side and walked over to what looked like a small wood stove. She shoved one of those precut logs that are already soaked in lighter fluid into the oven and lit it, followed by several other pieces of wood. In minutes, the already sweltering room became unbearably hot.

Tina removed the rest of her clothes, revealing her magnificent body, strong, muscular arms and legs, and flat stomach, wide hips, and a perfectly round ass, breasts like two small cantaloupes. A perfect body, glistening with a sheen of sweat that made her look like wet chocolate. If I'd still been capable of it, a body like that would have given me an instant erection.

"You asked me why I'm doing this," Tina said, walking back over and taking a seat in front of me. "Okay, fine. Let me tell you my story."

CHAPTER EIGHT

A HARD, ASS-KICKING, HO-BREAKING, SON OF A BITCH

"I grew up poor," Tina said. "You could've probably figured out that part. My momma was a ho too, a heroin addict. Sometimes did crack to get back up so she could work after nodding out on horse. She used to bring her nasty-ass tricks to our apartment at night. I'd be sleepin' on a mattress right there on the floor next to her bed while she was 'payin' bills,' as she called it. Which was funny because she was 'payin' bills' almost every night, yet we still got the lights or the gas or the water turned off every other month, along with eviction notices. All she was really doin' was payin' the dope man.

"They'd be gruntin', moanin', and sweatin' on that squeaky-ass bed, and she'd be tellin' me to just go back to sleep. But how the fuck was I supposed to sleep through all that? Especially through the violent ones. I'd hear 'em, smackin' Momma around. I'd see these cruel, dirty, sweaty men abusin' my momma in all the worst ways. I hated every last one of those motherfuckers, even the ones who were nice enough to bring a soda or a piece of candy for me. I'd smell their sweaty-ass funk or their cheap-ass cologne. It would make me sick. If I complained about anything, needin' sleep because I had to go to school the next mornin', being hungry or thirsty, or tried to stop one of 'em from hurtin' my momma, I'd get beat. Sometimes, I would go hide in the bathroom 'til it was over, but most of the time I'd lie there, scared and numb.

"Sometimes, the men would touch me too. If I cried or tried to run or fight back, I'd get beat, so after a while, I would just let 'em grope on me. I'd lie there still, like I did all the other nights when it was Momma gettin' fucked, and just wait for them to get their nasty hands off me. Eventually, they started doing more than just touchin'. I guess it was some kind of a kick for them to fuck a mom and her daughter in the same night, sometimes at the same time. By the time I was ten years old, Momma was sellin' more of my pussy than her own. It was the heroin. It had her ass. And when that horse git you, you'll sell anything you got for a fix, even your own child…"

I left home and hit the streets when I was twelve. Can you even imagine turnin' tricks before you've even started to bleed? I learned how to suck a dick before I could understand fractions. It wasn't long after I started hoin' that I got scooped up by a pimp. I guess there wasn't no way a young fine piece of ass like I was could stay independent for long.

My pimp was a hard, ass-kicking, ho-breaking son of a bitch. He scooped me up off the street after just a couple weeks. I was working a corner where two of his other hoes worked, and they tipped him off. He came rolling up in a white Mercedes E-class. He was wearing a white suit, no shirt. His chest muscles and six-pack abs were just popping out everywhere. I'm tellin' you, I had never seen a nigga that fine. He was prettier than I was. Tall, cocoa butter brown, shaved head, looked like an NBA player in black alligator shoes with dark shades on. His name was Johnson. On the street, they called him "Long Johnson" because he was, like, six-foot seven and because he had a nine-inch dick. He was about the finest, smoothest nigga I ever saw.

He asked me if I was hungry and then took me out to this nice fancy restaurant. He ordered for me: steak, lobster, crab cakes. I hadn't ever eaten food like that. I felt like the rich folks I saw on TV. Then he took me shopping for new clothes at all these fancy boutiques. I felt like a princess. After that, he took me back to his apartment and we started snortin' coke. Then he raped me for two hours. He took Viagra so he could keep going and made sure he'd stretched me out good. When he was done with me, he invited his other pimp friends over, and they took turns on me. The whole thing lasted maybe eight or ten hours. When it was over, he gave me a bath, made me douche both holes even though my pussy and my asshole was all torn up and bleeding, sprayed me with perfume, dressed me in some of them nice clothes he had just bought me—ho clothes, a short, skintight pink spandex dress and these glittery five-inch heels—then put my ass out on the corner. He told me I'd better make a thousand dollars that night and every night afterward or he would slit my throat and bury my body in the basement of the abandoned apartment building next door. I lived that life for seven years until I met Mitch.

Mitchell Taylor was about the sweetest man I ever met. He owned a tattoo shop on the strip, and I would just go in there and talk to him sometimes when I needed a break from all this shit. He was a big dude. Not tall like Johnson, but thick and muscular like a little tank. He said he used to wrestle and play football in high school and college, but dropped out of college and spent a few years in the military, Marines, I think. When he left the Marines, he decided to pursue his passion for art and somehow ended up gettin' into tattooin'.

Johnson didn't like me going in there talking to Mitch when I was s'pose to be workin'. He kicked my ass for it at least three or four times, but I liked Mitch, and I ain't have no other friends, unless you count them other jealous, hatin'-ass bitches in Johnson's stable. Them bitches hated me because I was young and pretty and pulled in twice as much money as them, so Johnson spent more time with me than with any of his other hoes. He would buy me bullshit little presents, cheap jewelry, and clothes he got from boosters. Anyway, them hoes wasn't any of my friends, but Mitch was.

When Johnson realized I wasn't gonna stop going to see Mitch no matter how much he whooped my ass, rather than damage his product and fuck up his money, he decided to talk to Mitch directly. That was a mistake. Mitch wasn't nothing to fuck with. For a white boy, he was hard as hell.

"Listen, white boy, if you want to spend time with my ho, you gots to pay like every other trick," Johnson told him, pointing a long brown finger like a tree branch, jabbing it in Mitch's chest.

Now, I hadn't ever seen Mitch get mad, but I saw the storm clouds in his eyes and knew thunder was comin'. He stood up from his chair, and Johnson just smiled at him. Johnson didn't think no short white boy had anything for him.

"Oh, you bad? You want some of me? Well, come on then, fool!"

Johnson carried a switchblade and a Smith & Wesson 9mm, but for some reason his dumb ass decided to make it a fair fight. Now, I keep callin' Mitch short, but he was actually about five-ten. Still, that's about eight inches shorter than Johnson, and Johnson had the reach on him. Mitch charged in, Johnson threw a jab and right cross, and Mitch ducked under both punches, grabbed Johnson just above the knees, lifted him off the ground, turned that nigga upside down, and dropped him right on his head. His forehead hit the tile floor and cracked wide open. Blood sprayed everywhere, but Mitch wasn't done. He climbed on top of him and started punchin' the shit out that pimp. He beat him so bad I felt sorry for him and begged Mitch to stop. I was afraid he was gonna kill 'im. Mitch stood up and took me by the waist, and he kissed me.

He hadn't ever done that before. He kissed me right on the lips.

Now, Johnson had always told me that he was the only one allowed to kiss me on my lips. Tricks could shove their cocks down my throat, make me lick their hairy balls and dirty assholes, cum all over my face, but they had better not kiss me or he would kill us both. But Mitch looked Johnson right in the eyes, pulled me close, and kissed me like we was long-lost lovers. Then he reached down and grabbed Johnson by the gaudy-ass Versace shirt he was wearing and lifted him off the floor like that pimp ain't weigh more than a pound. He pulled him close and spoke to him all sweet and calm like he was talkin' to a child.

"Now, we done with this bullshit, or are you gonna keep coming back here until either you kill me or I kill you, because Tina ain't your ho no more. You understand me?"

Johnson stared at him with the deepest, purest, darkest hatred I'd ever seen in anybody's eyes. It was like seein' the eyes of the devil himself. He reached for that gun in his waistband, and Mitch grabbed his hand and snapped his wrist like a popsicle stick. Johnson howled and screamed, and I swear there were tears in that nigga's eyes.

"We done now?" Mitch asked as he was takin' that 9mm out of Johnson's waistband and tossin' it toward the back of the store. I could see Johnson thinkin' 'bout goin' for that switchblade in his pocket, but he would have had to grab it with his left hand, and he wasn't good for shit with his left hand. He couldn't even finger me good left-handed. I saw the moment he gave up. I saw the quit in his eyes.

He nodded. "Yeah, we good. It's over."

"You sure about that? You sure you ain't gonna be comin' back here shootin' up my place, because if you thinkin' about doin' some dumb shit like that, it's best we just end this now."

Johnson shook his head and slowly climbed to his feet. "I

said we was good, nigga! You can have that tired-ass, dug-out, triflin', skank-ass ho!"

Mitch looked at him long and hard. "I know you probably make a lot of money off her, and I don't want you sittin' around thinkin' about all the money you lost and deciding to change your mind and come back for her, so how about I give you ten thousand for her right now? We can just call this a business transaction."

Johnson looked at him all skeptical-like. "You gonna just give me ten Gs for this bitch?"

"That's what I said. I been savin' up for a new Harley, but I don't really need a new bike. It's better spent keepin' the peace between us, right, brother?"

Johnson's nostrils flared like a bull. "I ain't yo' fuckin' brother! Just give me my money and you can have this bitch!"

And Mitch paid him. I couldn't believe that shit. Nobody had ever done nothin' like that for me before. I was worried he was gonna keep me as a slave or somethin'. I mean, Mitch had always been nothin' but nice to me, but you never know. I'd never seen him beat someone half to death before either. He could have been a psychopath.

Johnson left the shop, and I was just standing there lookin' at Mitch like he had a dick growin' out of his forehead.

"Why you do that, Mitch?"

He turned and looked at me with an expression that was both hurt and confused. "Tina, I love you."

I was shocked. I had no idea he felt that way or how long he'd had those feelins for me. We'd only been friendly for a couple months. What surprised me even more was that I kinda felt the same way.

"I-I love you too, Mitch."

He told me I didn't have to ho no more. That he would take care of me. I didn't know what to say.

"I don't need no man to take care of me," I said. It was what

I thought I was supposed to say, but the truest part of my soul yearned to be taken care of.

He reached out and stroked my cheek tenderly. "I know you don't. I know you don't need me. I want you to want me."

"I do," I said, and it felt like we had just gotten married. But I still had my regular clients, like you, and Mitch had just spent ten thousand dollars on me. I didn't want him to feel like he owned me now, so I told him I'd pay him back.

"I appreciate what you did for me, Mitch. Ain't nobody ever looked out for me like that, but I can't have that hangin' over my head, not if we're truly gonna be together. I have to pay you back so I don't feel like some property you bought and paid for."

Mitch nodded. He understood and said he respected me for that.

He didn't like that I was gonna still be sellin' pussy, but he knew what I was when he met me, and I promised I would quit as soon as I raised the ten thousand dollars to pay him back. You were my next client. Six months later, Mitch started gettin' sick. We were livin' together by then. I had stopped hoin', and we were even talkin' about marriage. I learned to cook his favorite meals and would clean his apartment every day and iron and fold his clothes and shit and pack a lunch for him just like those housewives on TV. I was happy.

"But then he got a cough that just wouldn't go away, and he started getting these spots on his skin. We were afraid he had cancer, and it was. Kaposi-sarcoma. He got it on his face, on his chest, legs, and arms, even in his ass. He didn't have health insurance, so by the time he went to the hospital and was diagnosed with full-blown AIDS, it was too late. They gave him antiviral medication, but they couldn't reverse it. He died a year after rescuing me from Johnson.

"And you killed him!"

CHAPTER NINE

BLOOD AND FECAL MATTER POURED FROM THE PIPE...

Tina's tears were more terrifying than if she'd been yelling or cursing or threatening me. Watching her sob for her dead boyfriend, I was certain all that pain would soon be visited upon me tenfold. She glared at me murderously, tears streaming down her face, all her pain and anger contorting her features into a rictus of hate. I tried to read her intentions in the hard lines, wrinkles, and furrows formed from her grief.

She walked over to where her knives, scalpels, saws, and hammers were laid out on the table and knelt to pick up a box. She then walked back over to the woodburning stove. I couldn't take my eyes off her, wondering what was inside. The confusion I felt when she removed the large pewter chess set from the box and began putting the chess pieces into a cast iron pot was impossible to keep off my face, even in the condition it was in.

"Mitch taught me how to play chess. He was really good at it. Never let me win. He gave me books on chess strategy, and I got better and better until I finally won. That same day he was diagnosed with AIDS. This is the only thing I have left from our time together. I sold everything else."

Tina put the cast iron pan into the oven and closed it. I had a really bad feeling about what she was going to use those superheated chess pieces for, but I'd begged and pleaded and apologized and made promises and even a few threats. There was nothing left for me to say. Nothing I could say that would have dissuaded her from whatever she was planning.

"You know I never got sick? You gave me AIDS, hepatitis, gonorrhea, syphilis, chlamydia, and genital warts, but I never got any symptoms. Not even a smell or discharge or anything. This herpes outbreak I got now is the first one I've had in years. The doctors call me a supercarrier."

"Super-spreader," I corrected her.

"Nah. That's you. I ain't spread this shit to nobody. I always wore a condom after Mitch died. I ain't care how rich, or handsome, or clean they looked. I always wore a condom. I made that mistake with your ass. You were handsome and always smelled good, and you always paid extra for it, so I let you fuck me without a condom. You were so fucking freaky, always wanting to eat me out after some other trick came inside me; it turned me on. Johnson always made me douche before he'd even stick his dick inside me, and he never went down on me. You licking other dude's cum out of me made me feel special. I guess I'm a sick motherfucker too. That don't mean I deserve what you did. You fucked me up. Fucked up my whole life with all them diseases you gave me. I'd never do that shit to nobody. I ain't like you. I ain't no disease spreader. That's you! That's what you are! You the damn super-spreader!"

I wanted to tell her again that I was sorry but knew it was a meaningless statement. Of course I was sorry now, with my lips and eyelids cut off, my testicles burned, and half my chest removed. I had never been more sorry about anything in my life.

"Anyway, so I was tellin' you about that story by Monica J. O'Rourke, 'An Experiment in Human Nature.' There was this scene in the story where these dudes have this guy tied up, and they melt down some metal, stick a funnel in his ass, and pour molten metal into his asshole. Then they stick a catheter in his piss hole and pour metal in there too. Wild, right? Can you believe a woman wrote that shit?"

I was shaking now, trembling from head to toe. The injuries I'd incurred already were sending me into shock, but it was the fear of what she'd just described, imagining molten metal being poured down into my urethra, that made the trembling start.

Tina walked over and tipped my chair onto its side, spilling me onto the floor. My arms and legs were still taped to the legs and armrests.

"I been thinking about how I'm gonna get something up in your asshole without removing you from that chair, and I came up with an idea."

Tina had the straight razor open again. She knelt down behind me and began cutting the bottom out of the camping chair I was attached to. I felt the blade slice a searing half circle from one ass cheek to the other as she cut out the seat of the chair, exposing my naked ass.

"You stay right there."

I watched her stroll back to the table and remove a sawed-off metal pipe and something that looked like a metal straw. There was no questioning what she was planning; she'd already revealed her inspiration. Her walk back toward me seemed to occur in slow motion, as if time itself had been wounded and was limping forward, dragging one moment into the next on injured and atrophied limbs.

I took several deep breaths, doing my best to savor and prolong this moment of respite from the torture, trying to drink in my remaining moments of life and allow it to linger on my tongue like a sommelier savoring a rare and expensive vintage of wine. I recalled each memory, tasting the sweet springtime notes of joy like the nectar of peaches and the cold creaminess of vanilla ice cream. The bitter, smoky hints of disappointment and the dry burn of pain swallowed in quick gulps like shots of whisky.

"You don't have to do this. I didn't mean to hurt you. I am so sorry about Mitch." I knew it was futile. My sobbing and begging was not even slowing her down.

"You keep Mitch's name out your nasty fuckin' mouth!"

She kicked me on the point of my chin as I lay there on my side. Darkness swooped in like manna from heaven, rescuing me from my torment. As I lost consciousness, I prayed to gods I never knew that I would never awake, that this nothingness would endure forever and I would simply cease to be. That Tina would have nothing left to torture but my lifeless corpse. I imagined her visiting all manner of desecration upon it, dismembering my carcass with her scalpels, razors, and saws. Tearing me apart with her bare hands in her fury at being denied her experiment in human nature. I even felt a few seconds of elation imagining I had thwarted her revenge, even though it meant my annihilation.

It didn't last long. I awoke screaming as my sphincter was hollowed out, the rectal lining ripped and torn.

My guts cramped and twisted with the brutal intrusion of the cold metal pipe into my anus, tearing through my anal canal, shredding the thin mucus membranes, and puncturing my bowels. Blood and fecal matter poured from the pipe like a backed-up sewer. I lost consciousness several times during the ordeal. I recall waking up to a searing pain in my urethra and seeing Tina forcefully jamming that metal straw into my limp penis, pushing it through the thin fibromuscular tube through which I ejaculated and urinated as blood and urine leaked from it in a steady stream.

I thought there were no screams left in me. My throat was nearly as chafed and torn as my rectum, but watching Tina walk over to the stove and return with the cast iron pot, filled with the pewter chess pieces she'd melted down into liquid metal, loosed a fresh volley of terrified shrieks from my over-taxed throat and lungs.

"I'ma make sure you can't spread no more diseases to nobody," Tina said as she began pouring the melted pewter into the lead pipe she'd threaded through my rectum.

The agony of the pipe's invasion was eclipsed a hundredfold by the soul-searing anguish of molten metal burning through my bowels, boiling tissue and organs. I vomited up a thick stew of my own steaming liquified intestines and organs. Once more, I prayed I would be dead before she could finish her persecution, and once more, my body betrayed me, stubbornly clinging to life against all reasonable hope.

I lost consciousness again, but the moment I felt her hands seize my cock, my eyes snapped awake. This time she held the pan over my penis—stretched taught over the metal straw, still weeping blood and urine—and attached a funnel to the end of the straw. She began to slowly pour the superheated liquid metal into the funnel. I felt the pipe in my cock heat up, burning the inside of my dick, searing the uroepithelium lining of my urethra to the hot metal. The pain did not stop there. The metal followed my urethra all the way to my bladder.

"I'm sorry," I managed to say one last time before darkness finally claimed me for good.

"Yeah, you's a sorry motherfucker all right. Rot in hell, you sick fuck."

CHAPTER TEN

THE FIRE BETWEEN HER THIGHS

His death did not bring Tina as much joy as his torture had. She felt hollow inside, missing the company of his screams and pleas for mercy. A crushing loneliness overcame her. As long as that perverted freak had been screaming for his life, the ghosts in Tina's mind had been quiet. She'd hoped to silence those painful specters for good with his death, but their distant echoes persisted. It hadn't brought Mitch back, or the future they might have had together. It hadn't cured her of AIDS or hepatitis or herpes. It hadn't made her tomorrowa any brighter. All it did was leave her with a tortured corpse to get rid of and no motivation to do it.

"Fuck it," she said. "His ass can stay right here."

She did her best to clean up the crime scene and remove any traces of herself but knew it was futile. Her pussy juice was smeared all over his face, and she'd probably left hairs and fibers everywhere. Her only choice was to burn it all down.

Tina looked around for things she could use to start a fire. She piled old newspapers, magazines, bills, receipts, and computer paper onto an old whicker rocking chair, then struck a match and held it to the mountain of paper. As it burned, she added more wooden furniture to it—desks, chairs, an old rug—until the flames reached the ceiling.

She took one last look at the man she'd spent the last several hours torturing. She still didn't fully understand what drove him, why he'd sacrificed his beauty, his health, his humanity, and, ultimately, his life to feed his twisted kinks. In the end, she'd begun to at least empathize with him a bit, even if she didn't understand. He was a victim. He'd been molested, raped, abused, and taken advantage of from the earliest age, before he'd evolved as a sexual being. His life had been defined by sexual deviance and pestilence, and he'd found a way to find joy in it. Maybe, she thought, she could do the same? What had he called her? A super-spreader? Maybe that was her purpose?

Perhaps that sick fuck had come into her life not to damn her with disease but to free her with it? To show her a new way, a new purpose. She was asymptomatic when it came to most STIs. Perhaps this was her life's purpose, the thing that would give meaning to everything she'd endured in her life? She could just go back to being a sick whore, or she could be something much more, not just a bug collector but a bug spreader, taking down all the cheating husbands and sadistic, misogynistic tricks with viruses and infections.

Tina smiled and walked out of the room. Behind her, the warehouse burned, but it paled to the fire between her thighs.

ABOUT THE AUTHOR

Wrath James White is a badass motherfucker who writes badass things for other badass motherfuckers.

He is the author of such extreme horror classics as *The Resurrectionist, Succulent Prey* and its sequel, *Prey Drive; If You Died Tomorrow I Would Eat Your Corpse, Hardcore Kelli,* and, most recently, *Rabbit Hunt* and *The Ecstasy of Agony,* as well as more than two dozen other novels, novellas, short story and poetry collections of Extreme and Hardcore Horror. He has cowritten books with Edward Lee, J.F. Gonzalez, Matt Shaw, and Kristopher Rufty.

Wrath lives and works in Austin, TX.

www.ingramcontent.com/pod-product-compliance
Lightning Source LLC
Chambersburg PA
CBHW041212150726

48006CB00016B/2217